For Sarah and Benjamin
~ J W

For George
~ T W

LITTLE TIGER PRESS
1 The Coda Centre, 189 Munster Road,
London SW6 6AW
www.littletiger.co.uk

First published in Great Britain 1999
This edition published 2013

Text copyright © Judy West 1999
Illustrations copyright © Tim Warnes 1999
Visit Tim Warnes at www.ChapmanandWarnes.com

Judy West and Tim Warnes have asserted their
rights to be identified as the author and illustrator
of this work under the Copyright, Designs and
Patents Act, 1988

Have you got my Purr?

Judy West

Tim Warnes

LITTLE TIGER PRESS
London

"Oh Mummy, Mummy!"
"What's the matter,
little Kitten? Why are
you crying?"
"Oh Mummy, Mummy,
I've lost my purr."
"You'll find your purr,
little Kitten. Just wait
and see."

"Oh Dog, Dog, have you got
my purr?"
   "Woof, woof," said Dog,
licking his bone.

"I haven't got your purr,
  little Kitten. This is my *woof*.
  Why don't you ask Cow?"

"Oh Cow, Cow, have
you got my purr?"
"Moo, moo," said
Cow, flicking flies
with her ears.

"I haven't got your purr,
little Kitten. This is my *moo*.
Why don't you ask Pig?"

"Oh Pig, Pig, have you got
my purr?"
   "Oink, oink," said Pig,
snuffling in the straw.

"I haven't got your purr,
little Kitten. This is my *oink*.
Why don't you ask Duck?"

"Oh Duck, Duck, have you got my purr?"
"Quack, quack," said Duck, splashing in the water.

"I haven't got your purr, little Kitten. This is my *quack*. Why don't you ask Mouse?"

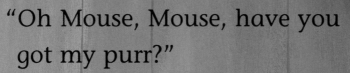

"Oh Mouse, Mouse, have you
got my purr?"
    "Squeak, squeak," said Mouse,
nibbling cheese in the barn.
"I haven't got your purr, little Kitten.
This is my *squeak*. Why don't you
ask Sheep?"

SQUEAK SQUEAK

"Oh Sheep, Sheep, have you got my purr?"

"Baa, baa," said Sheep, munching grass in the field. "I haven't got your purr, little Kitten. This is my *baa*. Why don't you ask wise old Owl?"

"Wise old Owl, have
you got my purr?"
"Hoot, hoot," said the
wise old Owl, blinking his
big round eyes.

HOOT
HOOT

"I haven't got your purr, little Kitten. This is my *hoot*. Why don't you go back and ask your mother?"

"Oh, Mummy, Mummy," wailed little Kitten. "*Nobody's* got my purr. Dog hasn't got it. Cow hasn't got it. Pig hasn't got it. Duck hasn't got it. Mouse hasn't got it. Sheep hasn't got it. Wise old Owl hasn't got it. Oh, Mummy, Mummy, I've lost my purr!"

"You haven't lost your purr,
little Kitten. Come here
and I'll explain."

"Nobody's got your purr.
Your purr is inside you
when you're happy!
Listen, little Kitten,
listen . . ."

"My *purr!* Oh, Mummy.
I've found my purr!
It was here all the time."
    So little Kitten curled up . . .
and purred and purred
and purred.

PURR

PURR